MW00942316

Now I Can
Read!

Long Vowel Sounds

A Little T-Rex Book

By Jeanne Schickli & Tara Cousins

Table of Contents

Book 1:

Brave Dave

I am Lane.

This is Jane.

Our dog is Dave.

2

Dave does not behave.

But Dave is brave.

At the lake,

Jane fell in.

6

She cannot swim!

8

Dave is brave.

Good boy Dave.

Book 2:

Pete and Irene

My pet pig.

I call him Pete.

2

My pet pony.

I call her Irene.

4

Come here Pete and Irene. It is time to eat.

A bowl for Pete.

A bowl for Irene.

Irene wants to eat what Pete eats.

8

Pete wants to eat what Irene eats.

9

Pete and Irene are happy.

Book 3:

I am Five

I am five.

I got a bike. It is mine, mine, mine.

I got a kite.

3

It is mine, mine, mine.

I fly it...

...in the bus line!

My kite! My kite!

7

I get my bike.

I go a mile.

I get my kite.

9

I smile!

10

Book 4:

Roses

I have a rose.

1

I have a hose.

I water my roses...

...with my hose.

4

I chose a rose to cut.

I have a nose.

6

With my nose, I smell the rose that I chose.

Look close at the rose that I chose.

See me pose with my rose.

The End

10

Book 5:

Flutes

I get a flute.

I make a tune.

You get a flute.

You make a tune.

We make music.

We are a duet.

Lula gets a tuba.

Bubba gets a drum.

Tom gets a trumpet.

Huey gets a horn.

We put on costumes and big hats.

We are a band.

We make music.

10

The End

Thanks for reading!

Visit www.amazon.com for the other two books in the **Now I Can Read!** Series:

Volume 1: Short Vowel Sounds

Volume 3: 5 Silly Stories for Early Readers

Made in the USA
Lexington, KY
09 October 2017